Helen Abrams was born in Upstate New York, in the town of Fulton. She moved to Claremore, Oklahoma, when she was six years old. She fulfilled her salon dreams with her own place in Claremore. Helen is married and settled down now in Broken Arrow, Oklahoma, which is 30 miles west of Claremore. She is a devout Christian of Assemblies of God. She still does nursing home ministry by doing their hair. Be excited as you go with her through the journeys of life.

Dedicated to my parents, Leona and Francis Abrams, and to my brother, Jim Abrams. God rest their soul. And Danny Nole, my supporter, friend and continuous helping hand. Nelson Abrams, I will always be thinking of you.

Helen Abrams

SINGING IN THE FOREST

AUSTIN MACAULEY PUBLISHERS™
LONDON • CAMBRIDGE • NEW YORK • SHARJAH

Ordering Information
Quantity sales: Special discounts are available on quantity purchases by corporations, associations, and others. For details, contact the publisher at the address below.

Publisher's Cataloging-in-Publication data
Abrams, Helen
Singing in the Forest

ISBN 9781638291633 (Paperback)
ISBN 9781638291640 (ePub e-book)

Library of Congress Control Number: 2022919661

www.austinmacauley.com/us

First Published 2023
Austin Macauley Publishers LLC
40 Wall Street, 33rd Floor, Suite 3302
New York, NY 10005
USA

mail-usa@austinmacauley.com
+1 (646) 5125767

I acknowledge the whole team at Austin Macauley Publishers.

Chapter One

I was seventeen. I was a blonde-haired, hazel eyed; five-foot seven inch; loner. I went to Adair High School. Four older sisters and one older brother. They attended Sequoyah School in the outskirts of Claremore, Oklahoma. Two-hour drive from Oklahoma City. They had lots of faults in their life and visited the office quite frequently. They never finished school. So in order for me to have a better life in school, we moved. Parents' choice.

I played basketball and track in high school. I was no good at any of it, most of the time in last place. I like the way it made me feel important even if it was only for myself. There was this one teammate I had and she really didn't care for me. I don't know why; I think it was because her dad and I got along really well after school. We rode horses together. We worked in the barn driving out every piece of dust that was in there. We did that quite often. He was like an uncle to me. I enjoyed that every day and she despised that. Well, that's my thought. One day, I was in the locker room because I was having a knee problem and every one of the girls who played on our team was on the basketball court. I got ready to leave the locker room when the girls came through the door. I stuck around for a moment hoping they would talk to me about something and the next thing I knew, the girl I told you about, well she accused me of stealing her $20 bill out of her back pocket. Having this event drew me closer to God. Vo-tech was my haven. I graduated in 1985.

I enjoyed singing. Thanks to my brother who taught me to sing in the forest no matter what comes. He said whenever you feel blue or you feel excited no one cares because you're singing alone to the universe and to God. This helps you to develop your inner spirit. I asked him what he sang and he said, "Elvis Presley." He was 13 years old.

So I began to make noise in the forest to Paul McCartney. I was nine.

After High School, I was trying to decide what was next. I was hired as a sewing machine operator at King Louis's in Adair, Oklahoma. I still lived in Adair with my parents. A few weeks after my job, my parents informed me that they have decided to get a motorhome and do some traveling. Soon they packed up and said their good-byes. Things were okay at first. I felt a little lonely and all my friends that I had from school moved away to find bigger hopes. I graduated from a class of 45 students. I continued working and found myself one day in the shower and had cold water. I thought that it was very quick for me to run out of hot water. I went and checked the water in the sink about two hours later. No hot water still. I called my parents and let them know about the situation. Mind you, I had no idea how to take care of a place on my own. Dad got on the phone and asked me to check the propane tank. I replied, "Is that the big white thing in the backyard?" He giggled and said yes. He helped me navigate around the tank, then asked me to read the meter. I found out then that it was empty. Mom got on the phone next and told me the company and phone number for the propane. I said that I would handle it. Mom said it would cost about $250. I told her I didn't have that kind of money. She giggled as she proceeded to tell me to reach between the wall and refrigerator there should be an envelope taped there. Inside was $300. She said she put that there before they left for an emergency. Bless them for looking out for their daughter as they always have. They were camped in Port Aransas, Texas. I was getting their mail and sending it to them once a month. At this time, Mom asked me why I was sending them the bills. I told her I didn't know what a bill looked like and I was waiting for them to come to me with my name on them. She informed me that they did not change the name on the electric or gas bill and any other bills that may come in from the house expense. So all along, my parents were still watching over me by paying the bills. At that time, my parents asked if they came home and got me would I go with them? I wish I would have gone now. Finding my freedom made me say no. Two months have passed now and I was still alone.

I had family that lived in Tulsa and Bixby, Oklahoma. I never contacted them during the time I lived alone because I didn't think they wanted me in their lives and they haven't contacted me all this time. I don't know how they feel about my graduating from high school. They said they were proud of me but all my life they've always treated me just a little differently than they did someone else. Or that might be what I think. Growing up, I can't remember very many special moments with my sisters. I had one sister who was very mean to me. It just so happened to be the one sister I shared a birthday with. She was eight years older than me. I was eight years old. She would chase me around in the yard and when she caught me, she would throw me down on the ground, sit on my belly and hold my arms down with her legs. Then she would proceed to pull grass from the ground and shove it in my mouth as I was yelling, screaming, and crying. She could have killed me. Another time my two other sisters decided to play truth or dare with me and dared me to take all my clothes off and run around the half-acre garden and come back to the house. I was nine years old. When I got to the door, they wouldn't open it right away. They would just laugh. My feet were on fire with the cold and of course, my whole body was shivering. Then we were playing hide and seek in the house and one of my sisters thought it would be a good idea for me to hide in the freezer. I survived.

Yet I still wanted to visit them.

One afternoon on Saturday, I heard a knock at the door. I went to the door and saw my sister Nellie. I invited her in and we caught up on subjects. During our visit, she asked me if I would come live with her in Tulsa. I pondered the question. I thought this might work out for the best. Within the next couple of days, I was on my way to live in Tulsa for a new experience.

On my journey to Tulsa I thought back of the time I was 12 years old. I met two wonderful girls, Cindy and Christy. During that time, I stayed overnight with them and I noticed their family was different from mine. They even prayed before we ate. I learned at that time about Jesus Christ my Lord and Savior. I wasn't going to church but only hanging with the girls did I learn some steps of obedience. Still not enough to know the choices in right and wrong and direction for my encounters to come.

When I went to live with my sister, Nellie, she had three children and divorced. She was only three years older than I was. It came about that I babysat for her often. She only came home about three times a week. I found myself packing lunches, getting kids dressed, and to the bus stop. This went on for a month.

One afternoon I was sitting in the front lawn of Nellie's house and looking through the clovers to see if I could find a four-leaf. A few moments later a gentleman came up behind me and asked, "Is this what your looking for?" In his hand was a four-leaf clover. I fell head over heels for the first time in my teenage life with Tom. We had a relationship for about six months. Then, our very first fight. We broke up (for now). During the time I spent with my sister, I was able to get acquainted with another sister, Rose. So after the argument, I went to my sister Rose's house. She had a nice home and a horse. I rode that horse often. I remember one day riding, I guess the horse didn't want me to ride her because it took off running almost as fast as it could and came across a tree and rammed my leg with my knee. Needless to say, I jumped off even though my knee was a little weak. Another time I was sitting on the porch with nothing to do on a Saturday. I was nineteen years old. She had asked me to go to the grocery store with her and I went. She introduced me to two young fellows and their sister that they knew from church. The next day, they came and picked me up and we went to a place by the water. We just sat and visited and then they took me home. It was nice to have people around me that were Christians.

Rose's family were churchgoers indeed and I seem to enjoy a peaceful moment in their home. They even prayed at supper time. I went to church with them. I was eager for a job.

Chapter Two

Our parents were home for the holidays. They were travelers. I truly love my mother. So as I was listening to the laughter, I began to mind play.

A Sunday afternoon with a family get-together,
we greet everyone like it's been forever.
All gathered at the kitchen table talking up a storm,
The kids are outside playing in the sunshine, so warm.
"Dinner is ready," our head cook would yell,
we all bow our heads to keep us from hell.
"Dinner was great," I told them all,
but I'm headed for the chair by the far wall.
Kicked back in the lazy boy the news talks about how things are getting worse, and the kids are arguing about who's gonna be first.
I closed my eyes and thought about where I went wrong or am I right?
Who can I talk to you, I need my friend to hold tight.
I see a lot of mess ups I have done in my past,
and one of the biggest, I didn't realize till last.
My eyes opened and I started seeking for my friend,
She's the one with an ear that listens and a hand to lend.

She always had my answers, love and understanding, that I needed when I was down and out; Her faith in me was great, when she says, you'll make it without a doubt.

Her heart was and always is understanding,

she brings me my share of comfort, never ending.

This girl is my friend, and she is not lost and doesn't need to be found,

for she's probably looking for me; her faith is within me, wherever I'm bound.

I always knew who my friend was she's the one who can forgive and forget,

and walk away smiling and not be upset.

I realize my friend is the best friend anyone could have in their life to share,

She has what it takes to love, listen and understand but mainly she cares.

Sometimes I can't help to wonder why she hasn't given up on me,

and then I remember her advice of hope, love and faith, how it should be.

My best friend noticed me watching and she gave me a loving smile enough to say,

Helen try leading the way.

Then I smiled wiped away some tears,

I know you have been trying to help for the last twenty years.

She smiled as a tear trickled down her cheek,

I whispered I love you and gave her a wink.

A smiled appeared across her face,

Family get-togethers there is no better place.

My mother and I share a special gift which will never end,

This gift is called friendship and my mom is my best friend.

Tom and I got back together. We moved in together. It is funny what teenage love will do. I didn't realize what kind of mess I got myself into. There were parties every weekend at our house and I really didn't know what was going on because of my lack of intelligence in the outside world.

I began to get scared. I had no job and no money. I didn't want to stay at my sister Nellie's house because they lived in the same atmosphere. Rose was too busy. So she said. I let her down. I realize that now. I could have left and gone to my parents' house but I had no money and no way to get the gas and lights back on. It never crossed my mind to reach out and ask for help from my parents.

As I sat there amongst the situation, I began to pray. I asked the Lord to help me get out of this place. I had been reading my Bible. A verse stood out to me. 2 Corth 1:10.

And He did rescue us from mortal danger, and He will rescue us again. We have placed our confidence in Him, and He will continue to rescue us.

I told Tom I needed to get a job. He wouldn't have anything to do with that. He was very controlling.

I prayed and I prayed and I started drawing pictures of angels, churches, and crosses. "I drew hope." I hung these pictures in the house. Again, I sat and started praying and reading the Bible. I did not know anything else to do. Seeking Jesus sometimes leaves you lonely. In my eyes anyway. I did not know better. As people were entering the front door, they were staring at me in wonder, what was she doing? I was accused of being a narc. With the chaos going on, the door coming open and the door going closed, so I got myself into a pickle living here.

Yes, Tom and I had many arguments and I got to escape once in my car but unfortunately, I was stranded on the side of the road, broken down. Luckily, I got my income tax return the day before and I used it to get my car towed and fixed. That was pretty much all my money.

Again, I was stuck in a house where I didn't want to be. Four months now, I was still 20. And then, it got worse in my life.

I had a chair that was my thinking chair that was out on the front porch. I retreated there. I heard the front door open and out came Tom. He was frustrated and angry. I'm not sure what about but he started yelling at me and hitting me. He went back inside and I sat there scared and afraid. I retreated then back into the house. Shortly a knock at the door came. Being frustrated about repeatedly getting up and down to answer the door, I just yelled out, "Come in!" Two police officers. Everyone scattered but me. I was the only one left in the presence of the police officers.

Bible in my lap, I proceeded to ask what brought them this way. They told me that there was a disturbance on the porch and the neighbors had called about it. They asked if there was anyone else that lived there or did I live alone. I told them I had a boyfriend. They asked if he was present. I got up from the couch, laid my Bible on the coffee table and I went into the bedroom to retrieve Tom from the closet. Coward. As I waited for him to come out, they gave me a look of surprise and I just walked past the police and went back to the couch and grabbed my Bible. They stepped outside with Tom and talked for a while and then left. At that time, I knew I had to get out. I left there and went to my sister Rose's house, not sure if she would have me. We had been talking briefly. There I stayed. I was delivered from the chaos. Again, my Savior delivered me from the hands of trouble, chaos and despair. Even now. Even me. I really didn't know much about the Bible and it was difficult for me to understand. But I learned from my sister. Matthew 6:2 Do not worry for hope is confidence.

I found myself singing in the forest.

Rose had Bible study every Thursday night. One evening, I witnessed someone speaking in another language. I asked questions and got answers. I knew a little bit more than I did before all my events happened. Baptism – to be saved and believe in Jesus. Baptism in the Holy Spirit – the eagerness to witness. I was hoping I was going to lead into the right way of life.

Misunderstandings – Roses family was separating.

I made a split decision to pack up my bags and move into college. My parents were there to help. I was 21 years old, 1989. My dad was a disabled vet and I had all my expenses paid for. I went to OSU Tech. Located in Okmulgee, Oklahoma. I did not know there were Christian Schools. I sat in my dorm room one evening and there was only one pay phone on that level. I heard two girls giggling and took a peek. When they were finished with the phone call and started to pass my door, I hollered out hello and they responded. I invited them in and we chatted about where they were from and what course they were taking. Just seems to have it they were taking the same classes I was and classes started in the morning. We all went together. We grew close together as a tight-knit threesome. We went everywhere together. Kathy, she made me laugh all the time and then Brittney would laugh and then I would laugh at her. They had friends that were nearby since their home wasn't far away from the college and we would meet up with some of their friends and have a good time. I don't know if every moment we spent together was a good time. Once we were at college and we decided to go to the lake. We had no car. A friend of Brittney's from school offered to take us to play frisbee. As we were leaving the park, a police officer pulled us over and found that the driver had been drinking. Us girls were in bikinis with shorts and we hadn't been drinking. The police officer checked us out and asked us if we had a driver's license. We didn't carry our purses so "no." He took us in and we spent three hours behind bars waiting before they let us go. We were being stared at and whistled at by prisoners. We weren't charged for anything but I think they were just trying to spook us. It worked. We did not speak of this to our parents.

Chapter Three

It was a Saturday night that I was spending time with Tom. He wrote to me several times saying that he had changed his life and gave his heart to the Lord. So I thought I'd give him another chance. He got a job immediately and was very friendly with my friends. I moved from my dorm into an apartment. One evening, I thought I would put on a party at the apartment. It was near the college. During the party people just kept showing up until I had about forty people in a one-bedroom apartment. Mind you, my apartment was upstairs. Soon the cops came knocking at the door and Tom answered it (Deja vu) he went outside and visited with them. I don't know how he got us cleared.

One week later, our responsibilities from my parents were to go to their house while they were gone on vacation and check their home. The drive was about an hour and a half away and we were happy for the drive. We got there and learned that everything was fine and we headed back home. We got into an argument and I asked him to pull over on the side of the road. I would walk the rest of the way. I really didn't think he would do that. He pulled over sure enough and I got out and he sped off. At this point, I was about forty-five minutes away from home. No purse. No phone. I thought about going the opposite direction and going to my parents' house but there were no lights or gas there. I began to walk in the direction toward my home in Tulsa. When he let me out, the location was on an overpass. Underneath this was the highway going straight to Tulsa. I decided to go to the highway and get there quicker. As I was walking, my bum knee decided to give me trouble. I stuck out my thumb hoping to get a ride. It was about fifteen minutes later when a semi-truck pulled over to the side of the road. He motioned me to come up. We greeted each other and he saw that I had been crying. He said, "Go ahead and tell me the story." So I began to let him know about my life with this man named Tom. He asked me if I was hungry and I passed. As I noticed we were in Tulsa, I began to explain to him that the next two exits we would be at my destination. A few minutes later, he passed the exit. I proceeded to let him know that he went too far. He smiled and said, "I have a place for you in Florida where you can be around horses and have fun with them and people would take care of you." I began to worry, yeah, a little late to worry. I began to strategize. I let a few moments pass and then I asked about a drink. He said he has some in the sleeper. I was hoping I wouldn't have a problem reaching back there to get one. I had a notion to just lay down and pretend like I was asleep. Thank you, Jesus, for insight. I knew nothing else at that point. I could hear the noise of the tires on the pavement. As travel went by into Oklahoma City, he pulled over for gas. He yelled in and asked if there was anything I needed. Having to use the restroom was out of the question. I just laid still. As he went into the store to pay for the gas, credit cards weren't a big issue I guess back then, so I made my escape. There were some bushes close by. I ran in that direction and hid behind some trees. I could see him inside the store looking in the women's bathroom and around the store. He seemed to have given up and headed to his truck again. I heard the engine start and he drove off. With no purse or phone, I didn't know what I was going to do about getting home. I stood beside the payphone and hoped that it would ring. A lady approached and asked if I was all right. I proceeded to tell her my story. She was very generous and gave me some change for the telephone call. She stood by me the whole time I was on the payphone. Of all people, Tom was who I called. I needed him to say I am sorry now. When I got off the payphone, I let her know it would be about two and a half hours before someone would come to get me. That was the distance between Tulsa and Oklahoma City. She didn't have that kind of time to wait with me. She informed me to go into the store and wait there. It would be safer. It didn't cross either of our minds to call the police. She was about fifty-seven years old. I know she was concerned for me and the main thing is that she met my money need. In need of a stranger; she was an angel.

Tom came to pick me up and he had two friends with him. He told me he turned around and came back to get me but I was nowhere to be found. I was quiet on the ride back. I retreated in my room till things settled down and nothing was mentioned more about my incident.

Chapter Four

I had an aunt and an uncle that moved here from New York to Claremore, Oklahoma right next door to my parents. My parents are home now. When summer came around my aunt and uncle could not handle the humidity so they said they wanted to move back to New York. They offered me their home and all I had to do was send the payments to them monthly. That was a great opportunity. Plus, I would be next to my parents, pregnant at 23 years old 1990. We moved immediately. I had two semesters left of college. I drove seven months pregnant back and forth an hour and a half three days a week to continue my schooling. Stopping to get sick at least twice. Last semester, I transferred to Rogers State University in Claremore and finished my degree. I remember one day in college I went to sit at the desk and I was too big to fit. It was a Monday and I fit fine last Friday. I was now a paralegal. Praises! It was May 1991.

Tom got a job at Jack Kissed Ford right next door to where we lived. He could walk. Which was good because we only had one car.

The time came for delivery, July 9th, 1991. When the baby was born, a son. I cuddled him and called him Lee. They would bring him to me. The nursery said that he would not eat and wanted me to feed him. He took the bottle for me. We got to come home with our bundle of joy. My dad, well he put a $20 bill in Lee's hand. "His first earnings," he said. I was twenty-four years old.

I found myself singing in the forest.

Everything went well for about a year and two months. I was making dinner and went out to the shed to get Tom to eat. I walked in and smelled marijuana and turned back around and went back in the house crying. He was going back to his evil ways. I began to pray. I told the Lord I would sell my soul to save our marriage. I found out later in life that the Lord Jesus, God Almighty hid my soul in the cleft of a rock for such a time to come. He came in and I told him he could either leave or stay and put that behind him. An argument began. I took Lee to mom's. I came back to finish the argument. He packed up some clothes and left. There went my relationship and there went his car and my son's daddy. I went over to my parents and they said everything would be okay. (They didn't like him anyway). My parents purchased them a new car and gave me their car they were driving at the time. They were always there for me.

I found myself singing in the forest.

I received my first "real" job since out of college. Suburban Chevrolet in Claremore, Oklahoma.

A gentleman came into the dealership and I recognized him. He recognized me. We began to talk and he told me about him being one of the people who came into Tom's house and saw me reading the Bible. He said I looked so peaceful amongst the storm. I said, "I don't know about being peaceful." He said that was the moment he changed his mind about what he was doing in his life and went back to his wife and changed his whole purpose. He said, "Seeing me reading the Bible and praying to the Lord and drawing my pictures led him to Jesus Christ." Just one life saved out of that chaos was worth it. God takes what the enemy meant for evil and He turns it for good.

There's always someone He is drawing near to Him. I was reminded again the Good Lord delivered me. God is good all the time and all the time God is good.

He will open doors for you. Even when you're in the darkest situation, He can bring you light and protection.

Any parent or (friend) who has a child in a situation such as mine, keep praying for them, keep seeking God for them. God will make a way when there is no way. I believe in miracles, I am a miracle myself.

Chapter Five

As I sat at my desk as a warranty administrator, I couldn't help but wander my thoughts to the time where I didn't have as much responsibility. A piece of paper was tossed onto my desk. Time to go back to work. I was the one who made sure all the claims for warranty were taken care of and the dealership was paid. After about six months there, I became the best warranty administrator in Oklahoma due to the stats. Marsha was at my door. I admired her so much. She's the one who taught me a lot of what I do here at work. She could have easily taken this job when it became open but she enjoyed being a service writer better. That's what got me here, her and my interview. I had a boss named Billy Ray Curtis. He was about 300 lbs. but he was harmless. We both shared the same office together. We always laughed and joked around and he complimented me a lot about how fast I was. One day, we decided to have lunch in the office. When we were trying to decide what we were going to have he suggested lobster. It was on him. Oh the envy of the people who passed by our window.

Our office was located in the shop and was sealed off with big windows in the front of them. We could see everything. I'll never forget the day when Billy Ray Curtis put my name on the door. I loved my job and I was there for five and a half years. Not long enough.

My other boss Mike Austin did a big favor upon me as well. Christmas bonuses were always good for everyone. They always had a great shindig for Thanksgiving.

A time came where Mike Austin sent me to a meeting in Tulsa, Oklahoma. The meeting was to learn more about warranty administration. But when I sat down in the class, it didn't take me long to know that I knew all about what they were talking about. I answered the questions left and right.

At break time, I went to sit down in the lobby and two men approached me and asked me questions about where I worked and then wanted to know if I would be interested in coming to work for them in Siloam Springs, Arkansas. That was about an hour's drive from Claremore. I told the two gentlemen I would not want to drive that distance every day. (Yes, I was considering it.) They were offering me $700 more a month if I joined them and the relocation fee. I got their phone number and said I would get back to them. Soon I visited with Mike Austin. I told him about my offer. He said, "I didn't send you there for you to find another job." He offered me $500 more a month if I stayed. I wanted to stay indeed, but I believed this was an open door. A door away from my old life.

How I can remember some stories.

My girlfriend Debbie was my best friend in the world at this part of my life. We would talk daily and we would see each other every day as well. She had a son my son's age. We loved the weekend bar life. We had a group of about seven to fifteen firemen who we all sat together by pushing tables together right in front of the stage and dancing. We would laugh and giggle and play pool and she would help me check out the new men. I always had one man in my life though, and that was my brother Jim. He and I would dance the night away. There was one dance, Old Time Rock and Roll. We would dance together and then one part of the song we would jump up on our toes with our cowboy boots on and dance like Michael Jackson. We had the dance floor to ourselves as people enjoyed the entertainment. Oh, how I miss my brother. He had passed away in an automobile accident and he was my best guy friend. Come with me as I show you how a brother is supposed to be.

The sun, shiny and clear, was the day upon us. I was nine, I had six siblings all older than I. Just three years apart. I had one brother Jim who is the kindest person I knew. Knowing the feuds I had with my sisters, he made me a little bedroom in his closet so I would be more comfortable. We would be together often. We had woods across the street from us and we had made several trails.

When my sister was present, she always wanted to scare me about a lake monster. I was terrified. She would wait till we got in the forest and then she would take off running yelling, "Lake monster, lake monster!" By the time I got to the house, I was exhausted but yet happy I didn't get eaten by the lake monster. My brother Jim always calmed me. He had built a tree fort twenty-five feet high. He didn't put a bottom step on the tree to climb up. I had asked him several times to do so because I couldn't climb and get in the tree fort. He refused kindly, but refused. I guess he wanted his privacy and he deserved it. I would stay at the bottom of the tree and play with sticks and stones and just wait for him to come back down. One day, my brother decided to let me into the tree fort. First, he pounded nails into the tree for a step. Then taught me how to grab the steps and pull myself up and go to the next step and do the same. Yes, when I got to the fourth step, I was a little scared when I looked down. Jim reassured me that everything would be okay. Just hold on to the steps. I arrived at the tree fort entrance. The door was at the bottom of the mansion, anyways in my eyes. I entered. He had carpet on the floor. A nice stereo system on the wall and one wall was plastic. He said, "To see the deer and other animals." I was astounded. I have never experienced anything like this in all my life. With my brother by my side, I felt safe. His messages of singing in the forest. My brother Jim was like Jesus to me. He was always kind, loving and accepting. He spent time with me. When I needed a hand up to a place that was beyond my reach? He always reached down, took my hand and lifted me to a higher ground. He was my rock.

RIP 1998. Dearly Missed.

Chapter Six

I needed a better life for me and my son now. So my intentions weren't just about the job, it was about finding a church, giving my life over to Christ, living for Him and raising my son in the right atmosphere, to what I thought it might be. I heard stories of my grandmother on my dad's side. She was the nun at one time. My grandpa told us that he went to a get together and he met her there. They both knew they fell in love at first sight. My sister Julie tells me she thinks that I missed my calling. The one thing that I remember is a prayer. "Oh Jesus, since I cannot now receive thee under the Sacramento Veil, I beseech thee with a heart filled with love and longing to come spiritually into my soul through the immaculate heart of the most Holy Mother and abide with me forever thee in me and I in thee, in time and eternity in Mary. Amen."

Setting at home one evening I began to drift off in my mind only to find me in the midst of a situation where God stepped through once again. I couldn't help but remember the day that He got me home safely. (College days with Tom.)

It was a starry night. One that I'd be grateful for if an event worked out differently.

Tom and I arrived at my parents' house to check on it every two weeks while they were on vacation. Checking the locks and making sure the windows were secure and not broken. Entering the home and making sure things were in its place. Being with the same deranged boyfriend while driving home, I was realizing the fear that I couldn't make it alone. At this point in my life, I was saved but was not fulfilling the life God had planned for me. I was a challenged child at birth. I was a little slow at catching onto things. So therefore knowing that I was with a deranged man didn't help me to get away from him at a quick pace.

While driving along Highway 44 near Tulsa, Oklahoma when an argument again broke out and it had to do with him changing his life so I may have a better one. I started the argument. He thought his life was perfect just the way it was.

As we were discussing that subject sometimes loudly, our car started to stutter. We pulled over to the side of the road and he checked out some things underneath the hood. He got back in and started the car and it had a hard time starting. I was quiet. It was then that he looked and saw that the gas tank was sitting empty. We were out in the woods area of the road. I began to pray and I prayed out loud, "Lord Jesus, I know that I am not perfect and I ask you for forgiveness of everything that I have committed in sin. I Glorify your name and I exalt you in the Highest. At this time, I'm in need of help. We are on the side of the road and in need of getting home. I give you praise and I thank you for all that you are. In Jesus name I pray, Amen."

Of course, Tom complained again about me praying. We discussed the Bible in an argument. After about five minutes, I yelled at him and said, "Just start the damn car!" It started and quietly we drove the rest of the way home which was about eighteen miles on an empty tank.

Thank you, Lord, for bringing me to my safety.

I found myself singing in the forest.

Chapter Seven

The day came for the move to Siloam Springs, Arkansas. My family was sad but excited for me. I already had my home sold very quickly. The relocation fee was all paid for which was $2,500. I bought a mobile home in a quaint little mobile home park near Walmart. It was a new home and I enjoyed the smell. Lee and I visited Walmart and he fell in love with a teddy bear. I bought it for him and he named it Fuzzy. Lee was four.

I started my new job. I knew right away that I didn't fit in with the people. They all stood standoffish. I was very nervous. I heard Arkansas people were a little rough around the edges. This is what I was going to be dealing with.

Well, after a week, I ventured out to look for a church. Lee and I roamed the town and found a church we would be interested in about two miles away from our home called Assembly of God. The following Sunday we attended. Lee went one way to his class and I to the auditorium. All the warm welcomes as I entered. The praise and worship were breathtaking. The message hit home. I found my place to worship.

After the service, I went to go find Lee. I found myself being stopped by several people to introduce themselves. A girl named Teresa introduced me to the Pastor. I made it to my son's class. He was the last child left in the room. The teacher introduced herself and said that she enjoyed having Lee in her class. I apologized for my lateness. Being new, there were several people wanting to introduce themselves, I told her. I found out they have a daycare!!

We were off for lunch and of course, he picked McDonald's, Fuzzy in hand. Then to Fayetteville, Arkansas. This was about thirty miles from our home. There was a recreational park that was named after the Jones who dedicated the place after their passing. They had swimming pools and tennis courts and everything you can name. We enjoyed our time as he played on the equipment.

The time came that we needed to head home. It was his naptime.

I laid down with him. I began a story of Jesus. How we see Jesus first with his arms open wide accepting us into the kingdom of God.

Calming him, I said, "Heaven is a beautiful place, with a lot of flowers. Visualize a field full of flowers that smell delicious Lee." I hesitated for his vision. Then a couple of seconds later, he said, "There goes a baseball."

As he was lying in bed falling asleep, I couldn't help but pick up a CD, "Point of Grace," my first Christian music purchase. I was hoping that the Lord would see my heart and find the time to reach down and give me peace in my soul. The time I needed that I was looking for when I was living in my hometown. No distractions now. The words of the music made my mind ponder things and get enlightened on others. Oh, how I heard how the blood that flows from the Cross and covers a multitude of sins. Oh, how I heard how glorious our Father is and His love endures forever. Oh, how I heard the suffering He did on the cross all for us. This just made me yearn more for Him.

I found myself singing in the forest right there.

Work went well. I knew my work so well that I could take a paper, run it through the computer and be ready for filing or for a customer to pay in less than three minutes. I found myself not doing much during the day because I was so fast. Nobody was leading me into what I needed to do when I was not busy. I was used to spending my free time goofing with Billy Ray Curtis. I went out on the floor of the service department and thought they would put me to work with writing up vehicle repairs but there wasn't any pulling in most of the time. Came time for an audit. All the paperwork that he needed to see was up in the attic. The temperature outside was ninety-seven. Therefore, the attic seemed twice as hot. As we went through the files, he found little error. When we finished our task in about five days, I decided that I wasn't done in the attic. I needed to clean this place out. They had files up here for fifteen years and we only needed to keep them for seven. I began to toss things right into the dumpster. The manager came out and asked if I knew what I was doing. I said, "Yes, you didn't need to keep all these records this long." He scratched his head and didn't know whether to believe me or not. Now I wasn't so sure either. But there they lay in the dumpster.

Chapter Eight

Christmas with my parents. Lee and I were ready for a road trip to see Grandma and Grandpa. I even wrote a little poem about it to share with them when I got there.

55 miles per hour? No, 70 for me,

because I had to get there by Christmas Eve.

700 miles to Port Aransas,

I can't wait to see their smiling faces.

Finally, I'm here! 4:10 in the morning,

Across the ferry, Port Aransas, the beach, is this it? It looks boring.

Christmas Eve morning as I drove through town,

no Christmas lights were shining, and no one was around.

Got to their house, but no one was up,

on the table was a note under an empty coffee cup.

I picked it up to see what it was,

"Dear Santa," I am writing to you because,

My daughter is not here,

So for Christmas, I want her Christmas cheer.

Without her Christmas wouldn't be the same I would say,

so Santa let her be on her way.

I will stay up waiting just a little longer,

then fall asleep and let my dreams wander.

Well Santa I know on Christmas Eve you're a busy man,

But let's take a little time to understand.

The Lord, you, and I can make my Christmas wish come true,

So let's bow our heads before Christmas comes adieu.

Thanks again for the times we share,

and Merry Christmas. Love the ones that care.

I laid the letter on the table as I made my way down the hall,

knowing that The Lord, Mom, and Saint Nick gave it their all.

I looked into the bedroom where my parents were fast asleep,

wondering if I should wake them or just take a peep.

I walked to the bed and gave Mom a jiggle,

she woke as I said Merry Christmas, then we heard a giggle?

We jumped to the window and up in the sky.

It was Santa wishing us a Merry Christmas as he was waving goodbye.

Their motor home was parked right on the beach. They were running power through a generator. It was good to get up in the morning and literally see the ocean right in front of you. Dad spent most of his time playing with Lee and riding bikes up and down the beach. Mom and I did nothing except talk. We talked about the Lord and I only knew a little at this time. She had asked about receiving the Holy Spirit, the subject that I had been talking about for months. This is what we did to make this possible:

It was a night that I will never forget. Before I left, I was an example of a true Christian to them. She was curious. They saw me in awe of God. We had spoken of the Holy Spirit in the past. She asked to receive it now.

Later, I saw a vision of me wrapping a present. So I found a box and paper. Put a note inside that read; "you just received the Holy Spirit." I gave the gift to Mom. Yes, it seems simple but when you're ready to receive something from the Lord do you know that all you need to do is just ask? It should be that simple and it is. Except that. Something I am still learning myself.

Today she had a glow about her. She was now a prayer partner. This gift was one of the best events I ever witnessed. We broke the chains of generational curses.

His power moves mountains and plants them beside the still waters.

I went for a drive.

I found myself singing in the forest.

The time came to leave and go home. The ride was wonderful. We had stopped at a place to eat on the way back and when I got in the truck, I told Lee we had to hit the road. He laughed and got out of the truck and literally hit the road. We entered Tulsa, Oklahoma. As I was driving along, Lee was asleep.

I had a feeling of rejection that I developed in my own thoughts.

As I huffed, I turned the radio on for a distraction. No matter what tune was on the radio, I just couldn't keep the beat in my mind. I started praying to the Lord Jesus Christ in heaven. (No, this is not a Jesus Take the Wheel situation but kind of.) I was coming through Catoosa, passing the last light when I suddenly had an informative call to pull over to the side of the road. A God call.

Of course, I questioned it for a moment and I heard it again. I slowed down and examined the side of the road, switched my blinker light on and I pulled over. By the time I came to a complete stop and put the car in park, I suddenly felt the notion again. This time to pull back out into the traffic. Blinker and accelerating, I was approaching the intersection where 412 meets Highway 66 and combines to 44. I saw a tractor-trailer and a car in an accident. It just happened and then it crossed my mind that it could have been me. Thank the Lord Jesus for speaking to me at the right time even amidst my storm to help me to regain my direction.

Chapter Nine

The following Sunday came and I was so excited about going to church even Lee was excited. Teresa met us at the door and she was so excited to see me again. This time, we sat closer to the front. The service went well speaking that the House of the Lord can change the heart of people through prayer and supplication. "We can move this city." At the end of the service, they had an altar call. I entered the front, got on my knees and lifted my hands and surrendered. I was 28 years old. Pastor came by and prayed and he asked me if I had ever been saved before. I said, "I was a young girl."

As I left there with a spring in my step eager to have a new relationship with Jesus Christ, little did I know that the joy would soon be challenged.

I loved children and was eager to start my new Wednesday night Missionettes Stars class. It was the age nine through eleven in my class of girls. One of my girls was Tiffany and she was eleven. Five weeks into teaching, I realized that Tiffany wasn't in class one evening. She seemed to enjoy the class very much and it concerned me that she wasn't present. Two Wednesdays later, she shows up. She called me to the side and was a little sad. She proceeded to tell me she was pregnant. I kept my cool and hugged her and let her know things would be fine. We prayed together and then I heard her story. She says it was a friend of her brothers. Time went by and we found out that she kept the baby and lived with her parents. I taught the girls a skit and we performed it in church service for the adults. One time, we got together for a sleepover at my house. We had so much fun. Just then, it was time to go to sleep. I put the shaving cream on one girl's nose and she woke up, touched it and wiped it on the next girl and this went on from girl to girl till they were all awake and we told stories again.

For such a time as this, I was glad to see that I had the savings in my account. I went to work that day and was fired. "Fired because of my skill that was too good for them," I said out loud. I went home and cried.

I sat around the house for the first couple of days. I found out about a job at a nonprofit organization that needed a receptionist. They were only offering three days a week. I was eager to start and hoped that it would go full-time. My job consists of account payables and handling all the food that came through the door. I counted it and stuck it on each shelf where it belonged. People would come in needing food and bills paid. I would assist them. It was a very rewarding job. In three months, I had to move on for a bigger paycheck.

I called my old boss Billy Ray Curtis and asked about my position. He said it was always open to me.

While my parents were gone for the whole winter months, I called them and asked if I could stay at their place for a short time, until I got my own place and sold my home.

They were excited and agreed to the terms. I took time to prepare for the move. Lee was excited that he was going to be back by his grandpa's side soon. Fuzzy rejoiced too!! I had boxes all over the house where I was already beginning to pack. My church family was saddened but yet prayers were with me. I WAS COMING HOME!

Chapter Ten

I went back to work and was driving back and forth from Siloam Springs to Claremore. I wasn't ashamed of leaving the business and going to Arkansas because I got the best gift there that anyone could ask for, Jesus Christ. I was so on fire for Jesus that I wore a dress every day because I thought that's what a Christian did. I hung up a cross over my desk behind me. People could see that I had changed. A married gentleman, David was a Christian. He was one of the mechanics. He would come to visit me in my office from time to time and we talked about the Lord. I was glad to have a friend at work that I could relate with. Even Billy Ray Curtis saw a big move in me. He wasn't harsh on me but he was interested in my behavior. Lee was riding back and forth with me and going to a daycare in Claremore. God was good to me once again.

As I was there, I asked about Mike Austin. I was informed that he had passed in a motorcycle accident. Hard for me to believe. I'm going to miss him.

During that time, I have found myself overwhelmed and I don't know why really. I left the business that day and went to my parents' house. My boss, Billy Ray Curtis came looking for me. He wanted me to come back to work and that he was sorry that it got overwhelming. I got up and left with him back to work. I was challenged.

Two days later, Lee and I went to another great place. We used to go to a big hill that you have to climb to the top and the road was in the making of a four-wheel drive. Just so happens that I had one. We would climb up that hill all the way to the top and we would sit up there and look at the view. One day, we had a picnic lunch. And we visited another great place in Arkansas in the summer. It was called Flint Creek. It had a nice pool area of water that you could swim in. Also you could go down below the waterfall and swim. Had a cliff to jump off. Both were popular places. Lee wasn't feeling good. So we went home and I took him to the doctor the next day.

Lee developed mono. As a mother, there was nothing I could do about it but just be comforting. His neck looks like a football. He didn't complain and he didn't act like he was in any pain. I've never had mono so I don't know what it would be like at all. God bless him.

A time came for helping our family. Struggling to make ends meet due to my relatives being unemployed. Helping them was making me have to budget clearly. I could feel the financial tension. I volunteered my time in church and Community. I prayed I would not show my concerns. I was praying for my family members to get saved. I learned sometimes the hardest part of helping the unsaved could be challenging. Cold-hearted, greedy, unappreciative just to name a few. Then the oh so easy, the grateful. I have learned to appreciate them both.

During volunteer day at a nearby kitchen, there was a lady named Twila who touched my heartstrings. Not to show favorites she sure showed favorites with me. Her many, many stories I hold in my heart even today. She was doing everything she could to keep her family in a home. I learned about humility with her and she taught me a part of it every day I saw her. A twinkle in her eye and a hop in her step, her smile crossed my mind.

About a month went by and we were still spending time helping our relatives. My financial struggle was becoming overwhelming also. On a Sunday morning after church, I went to the altar to pray. A lady about ten years older than I came up and asked if she could pray with me. Afterwards, I left for the foyer and then a gentleman came up to us and greeted my son and I. He reached out to shake my hand. I felt him slide something into my palm. He walked to the next person. I looked into my palm and behold, a $100 bill. I turned and looked at my son with love and said, "We are on our way to the gas station." There are so many blessings in this world that don't even pertain to us. Such as the gentleman who was blessed just by giving.

Humility – a modest or low view of one's own importance, humility.

Please be willing.

Chapter Eleven

It was Valentine's Day at work and I was doing just fine. Three girls received flowers and I was very happy for them. I had no one courting me and I got lonely on this day. I picked up Lee from daycare and headed home. Did the normal routine and when it came to bedtime, I prayed. "Lord in heaven, how wonderful you are. I know you love me and I love you. I thank you so much for looking out for me. I thank you for keeping my son safe." So on and so on and so on. At the end of my prayer, I told the Lord that I was lonely and I would have loved to have received flowers as the rest of the girls had. I cried a little and then laid my weary head down on the pillow. The next morning, I was getting myself and my son ready for work. My parents' home had a screened-in front porch. There was a hand lock on the inside and on the outside of the door when you were leaving. You had to put a padlock on it. As we walked out of the door, I turned quickly to lock the door as Lee was getting into the car. I felt something bump my foot so I looked down and there was a rose. I cried and thanked the Lord above for sending me a rose. Nothing came of that rose as far as a courter but I know for sure that the Good Lord wanted to make sure that I was loved, cared for and mainly protected by the man upstairs.

Lee was ready to go to school. Oh, the first time he got on the bus I chased it down waving goodbye. My little boy was growing up. We had started a new church, the Assembly of God in Claremore. I wasn't embarrassed to sit in the front row with my son and my niece and praise and worship the Lord during service. At the end of praise and worship, the pastor entered the pulpit, began to talk some and then said it's good to see the new people come in and be praising in the front row. I was appreciative and embarrassed. After church again, several people came up to me and introduced themselves. Even the Pastor came and did the same. I was invited to lunch with some ladies and I took them up on it. We sat and visited, mainly I listened and then lunch was served. Lee came along with us and he enjoyed some spaghetti. I enjoyed being with the ladies and getting to know them. I thanked them for inviting us. Lee and I returned home. I called to ask if I could help with nursing home ministry. I was feeling encouraged.

I found myself singing in the forest with Lee.

I put some Christian music on and I got out my microphone and began to sing along. Before long, I was buying karaoke and I was singing along with my microphone. Even Lee would engage.

It was good to have my desk back at work and my work coming across my desk. It was also good to share an office with Billy Ray Curtis once again. I love that guy. His wife would say "I'm his wife at home and you're his wife at work," that was funny.

I attended church on Wednesday night.

With the nursing home Ministry, you went to the nursing home and set up a small pulpit and the people would come down to the room and I would have praise and worship and a small message. After a few visits, I was getting familiar with the names of them.

As I went to get some people, some use the restroom first, some not sure. As I made my rounds, there was Paul. He was blind. He was headed in the right direction as he held the side railing. I told him I would be right there, keep going and we will meet together. I proceeded to enter Sally and her husband John's room. They seemed to be saddened. Crying. "May I ask what happened?" They told me that they just lost their son and said that they gave permission for my visit. I wept as well. I knew this couple well. I tried to comfort them and prayed with them. I began down the hall looking at my watch. I have been busy now for forty-five minutes. Teaching across a pulpit most times fell upon sleepy ears but I believe this time of their waiting was going to be understood. I carried my heavy equipment inside and prayed today would be the day of movement.

I have heard my pastor preach the same sermon and always seemed to attract new people that would respond. Today I would teach the same sermon, Healing.

The next time the staff had already gotten the residents, they were all in place. I greeted them all personally. About fifteen of them. I then began with a song of praise. "We Bring the Sacrifice of Praise and the Old Rugged Cross." The residents enjoyed it very much. Lee was only six years old. Then Lee would sing *It's a Good Good life.* We kept the praise and worship traditional so the residents could sing along. Then gave the call of rededication. I asked if anyone needed healing. Pearl was first to raise her hand. I went to her and asked what we should pray for. She wanted to walk. I asked the assistant if this was possible to perform. He assisted me. Pearl walked seven steps. Then Jerry. Same effect only nine steps. This went on with each resident. What a glorious moment. Linda hasn't walked in nine months but today, she did! As I left to drive home, I wept. Keep the faith I thought, just keep the faith.

The drive to my parents' house to work Monday through Friday became very familiar. It was so familiar that it seemed shorter. We would even stay the night at times. When my parents were home my dad was so happy to see Lee and they were gone out of sight most of the time. My mother and I would usually just talk and maybe go catch a bite to eat. My parents would also come and stay with me while waiting to sell my home. They stayed one Christmas with us and I enjoyed that very much. I remember Christmas Eve after I sent Lee to bed that I got him some toy soldiers and I was getting them together and putting them under the tree. I was trying to set them just right. Lee with Fuzzy came out of his bedroom and saw me under the tree playing with his toys. He said, "Mom, Christmas isn't till morning. How did Santa get the presents here already?" I just responded by saying he was a little early this year and he had so many people's houses to stop at. Thank goodness, I got away with that one. The rest of the evening, we sat around playing cards rejoicing with my parents. They stayed for two more days and then they were on their way home.

It was a stormy day of February. I was visiting my parents and everything was fine when all of a sudden, my dad began to have chest pains. We hurriedly called the ambulance and waited patiently.

I was deeply saddened. Lee was at his other grandparents' house. When the ambulance arrived, they quickly assessed the situation. Oh how they worked so diligently. They put him on a bed and out the door they went.

I drove my parents' car as Mom rode in the ambulance.

We arrived at St. Francis hospital in Tulsa, Oklahoma. In the emergency room, they took him.

Depression – I hate how it slips right into my life even when my skies are bright.

I began to pray.

Not knowing about certain things your body can do in 'time,' I heard the Lord speak to me that my dad would be alright and he has grown new veins.

Not really knowing what that meant I was reassured that my daddy would be alright.

A surgery was on its way as we were waiting for its arrival. I asked my dad if I could pray for him. He kindly accepted.

"Oh our precious Jesus, Father in Heaven, we come boldly to your Throne and ask your mercy to forgive us of our transgressions. Turn us from sin and cleanse us as white as snow. Oh Jesus, we thank you for that."

"I also ask in Jesus's name to heal my daddy's heart."

(Right then, I felt and heard the unction to pray out loud about what I heard in my last conversation. So I continued praying) "Jesus, I ask you to grow back new veins to make him whole. Yes Jesus, new veins. I pray that you guide the hands and mind of the doctors to take care of my daddy during surgery."

As I finished the prayer with my dad and mom, I bent down and kissed my daddy's forehead and told him I loved him very much. I told him a joke for him to lighten up a little bit and find some cheer in his heart before the surgery.

This country couple have been married for fifty years without one argument. They were out on a ride when the woman's horse started to act up. She got down from the horse and went to the front. Looked square in his eyes and said, "That is one." A few moments later, again she got down and glared right into the horse's eyes and said, "That's two." The third time she went to the front of the horse pulled out a pistol and shot it right between the eyes. The husband responded, "Honey, you can't just shoot the horse." She looked at her husband and said, "That's one."

He got a chuckle.

They came and wheeled him away. Mom and I sat and talked, and ever so often, we stayed quiet during the time he was gone.

He arrived back in the room and was asleep. He didn't quite get awake after his recovery visit. Again Mom and I visited and were somewhat quiet until that moment when he woke. We asked how he was doing and he said, "Okay, except I feel a pain in my chest and I believe it's from the opening that they made to get inside." Soon a doctor arrived to give us an update.

He explained to us that everything went well. He then explained how veins can grow back when there is a blockage. Your dad looks very well with his veins. They seem to have made a route around the blockage. He proceeded to inform us of other things that needed to be done and things that happened. My mom had questions also. He was very good at staying with us and making sure we had all of our questions answered.

When he left the room, Mom and Dad and I rejoiced. I sat by myself while Mom and Dad spent some time together. I pondered the situation about my enlightenment. The Lord spoke and told me, "That it was about the veins and building my daddy's faith in the Lord by hearing and receiving the Word of God." At that moment, I smiled knowing my dad and my Lord met in a mysterious way. Our Father can use your prayers for someone else to build their faith, not just yours. Here again my Father in heaven showed His miraculous healing signs and wonders as well as love, kindness and understanding. He will never fail you or forsake you and He will always hear your prayers and do what he intends to do to change the hearts of someone dear. I ask you not to think lightly of what the Lord can move in your life.

I found myself singing in the forest.

As time went by, my father got stronger and stronger. He couldn't wait to play with Lee again. Two months later, Lee developed a flaw in his eye. When he was watching television, one would draw closer to the other. We went to see an eye specialist. The doctor stated that he needed to have surgery on that one eye that would straighten out his vision. We explained this surgery to Lee and of course, he took it very well. Time came for his surgery. We were in the room with my parents and I noticed him acting a little funny. Funny to watch.

The anesthesiologist told us that he has already given him some medication to help calm him before the surgery. The surgery was a success and he needed to wear glasses for a while to help further correction in his eyesight. Lee did very well at keeping his glasses on. He even had to wear a patch at times. As a mom, I was very hurt to see this happening to my son. But I would not show it.

After his healing, we continued with our nursing home ministry. Lee would learn some songs with me at home and we enjoyed singing together.

Church came around again. It was my time to do a special on the stage. As I looked around the crowd as I sang, I noticed a white figure standing behind a girl. I didn't quite know what that meant. I sought the Lord all week and hopefully found this answer. Next Sunday, I saw the lady coming into the church and sitting down in one of the pews. I went over and found a seat next to her and sat down. Church hasn't started yet so I introduced myself and she also introduced herself as Nicky. During praise and worship, she got up and left the sanctuary. When the sermon started, she entered back in and sat beside me. After church, we visited in the foyer and I asked her where she worked, how many children she had, if her family lived nearby and did she live in Claremore. I also exchange my information. I asked her if she would like to join me for lunch. Oh, she declined.

As the week went by, I couldn't help it, I had her on my mind and prayed for her often. I hope that I will see her on Sunday.

Sunday came and I met her in the foyer and I asked if I could sit next to her again. I did and as praise and worship started, she again got up and left the sanctuary. She came back in for the sermon. That Sunday, we exchanged phone numbers. On Wednesday of the week, I gave her a call and asked if her week was going well. We spoke a little bit but only enough for a five-minute period to go by.

Sunday rolled around again and I sat next to her. The same ritual happened again with her leaving and returning. After church, we met in the foyer and visited for a while. On Wednesday, I called her and asked her what she was doing on Friday afternoon. She said she was free. I asked her if she would like to meet somewhere and have lunch, she told me she had no car. I said, "I don't mind, I'll come by and pick you up, what's your address?" Friday rolled around and I was so excited about going and visiting with her. I picked her up at her home and we went on the backside of Claremore Lake and found a nice little spot by the water and enjoyed each other's company. She proceeded to tell me her past and the reason that brought her to church. She had been in a cult. I didn't feel scared which most people would. I felt this warm feeling inside me, a warm feeling of love. I just reached over and hugged her and told her that we all care for her in the family of God. I asked her if I could pray for her and she didn't hesitate. First, I said, "when I say I will pray for you, it isn't because I am forcing my religion on you, it is because I believe in God and the power of prayer, and just because I care. Heavenly Father, I come to you with my sister Nicky, who has not met you as the Lord and Savior and she would like to have you come into her life and help her know what love is, thank you for accepting her." I said the sinner's prayer with her as well. We got into the car and I drove her back home. As I left, I started to weep, knowing her new life would be full of promise.

I found myself singing in the forest.

I called my choir leader and asked if I could do a song, a special on a Sunday morning. Sunday came and I saw Nicky come into the church and I greeted her. I didn't have to ask this time to sit with her, she offered. As the Church began with praise and worship, she left the sanctuary. I went to the foyer to speak with her. I let her know that I would be singing a special. I was hoping when I got up on stage that I would see her in the audience. When I was on the stage, I looked around for her and saw her sitting in her place.

I have been thinking all week about what song I was going to sing, and then I knew. It was on my heart and I sang the song No Stones to Throw by Seirra. This song I chose for Nicky. In this song, it's talkin' about a girl named Maggie but I changed the name to Nicky. I came back and sat with her when I was finished with my special. She reached over and squeezed my knee. After church, we met out in the foyer and I asked her to go to lunch with me. She accepted. The next time we got together was Tuesday. We went back to the same spot at Claremore Lake. We chatted awhile and I couldn't help but ask why she left the sanctuary during praise and worship. She told me that she feels like it bothers her so much her ears hurt, her stomach turns and she gets sweaty. She says she just goes out into the foyer. I explained to her that she was feeling those thoughts because the devil's lying. We prayed together for strength to get through this and that Jesus meets her right where she's at.

The next Sunday, the event happened the same as it has in previous Sundays. Except this time, I followed Nicky out to the foyer. As she was standing by a wall, I saw her shaking and I went up to her. I laid my hands on her shoulders and I commanded the devil to come out of her. I commanded the spirit not to be playing havoc with her. They had no place here. She began to weep and the shaking went away. I told her every time you feel this if it comes upon you, just tell yourself that in the name of Jesus, Satan you have to flee. Get your Bible and just hold it. Heck, one time I heard Kenneth Hagin say just stand on your Bible because you're standing on the Word. From that day forward, she enjoyed praise and worship and I enjoyed our friendship. Some Christians in that building didn't want anything to do with her. They didn't even greet her when she first started church or any day after that. Yes, they may have known some of her background but that gives them no right to throw stones. She's now a lover of Christ and I am blessed to be her friend.

My home sold. I had plenty of help with the church family and my family. The hardest part was moving my hot tub. I moved it right to my parents' home. My father enjoyed it daily. He said it helped his arthritis. Plus, he likes to play in it with Lee.

Chapter Twelve

It was a new day and work was going well. Billy Ray and I were connecting again with our relationship. Others were beginning to accept me, again.

I was invited to a church event by Brad. It was a Halloween hayride. I went as Tigger and I was the only one in costume. As I was getting on to the hayride, I noticed all the seats were taken except one by Brad. People giggled as they force this arrangement. I went along. I was quite attracted to Brad. We dated three times. All three times, we spoke about the messages from the sermon. I was thinking this is the fella because I enjoyed hearing the Word and we both enjoyed speaking it. Four weeks went by and he proceeded to tell me something that I needed to know if our relationship was going any further. Mind you, I'm a little short of a happy meal French fries if you know what I mean. My elevator doesn't go all the way to the top. It takes me longer to catch things than anybody else. I don't see danger in my life when it's right in front of me. He proceeded to tell me that he had been married before and he was going through a divorce, technically so was I. I was still healing from Tom. I didn't even know what all this meant but I pretended like I did. I was already falling in love. He excused himself so I could think about things. My second thought was he was in church and God gives everybody a second chance. So I believed that everybody should give everyone a second chance. Even in some cases he gives you a third a fourth and a fifth chance. I needed that. Plus, he talks about the Word all the time and how could he be going wrong? I began to pray for myself daily. Discernment for one.

One day, I was thinking about Brad. I went over to my parents to stay the night. It was cold and snowing. I was outside talking on the phone to get some privacy. When I was on hold, I asked the Lord for direction. "Help me with a sign to know what to do." As I continued on hold, I was walking up and down the side of the street in front of my parents' house. I saw something blue sticking out of the snow. I pushed down my body and picked it up. It was a door from a 'Tikes' toy truck that said RESCUE! I fell on my knees and I thank the Lord for insight. He gave me a sign through a door of escape and he rescued me. Rescued me from fear. Made me stronger. I was then freed of discomfort. Brad and I had our first fight. It was due to another girl who was interested in Brad. I should have let her have him then. This feeling made me feel like I was scared to death but the Lord heard me and gave me peace. Thank Jesus for always lifting me up when I am low. For always guiding me when I am lost and for always loving me when I don't feel loved.

Chapter Thirteen

When I was in high school, I took a course in cosmetology. It was mainly because my friends from Sequoyah School could go to the same Vo-Tech. Show up three times a week for three hours. I got to spend time with my friends and learn a trade. I remember one time my teacher asked us to do a long-layered haircut. Without looking around at anyone else, I stayed engaged in doing my task. When I finished, I turned to find the teacher and show her my work. She came over with awe in her eyes as she looked at my pretty much bald-headed mannequin. Then she giggled a little and the other students began to notice. This was an embarrassing moment of my life but my teacher turned it into something great. She displayed my mannequin in the window and the haircut was perfect. It just was too short for what she was asking. My relationship with her turned into my mentor in more than one way.

Two years and six months was my second time working at Suburban Chevrolet. I decided to venture out to do hair and get away from the car business. Billy Ray Curtis took another job two month earlier. I took my first job at SmartStyle located in Walmart. I was a little slow at first but I enjoyed doing hair so it didn't take me long to pick up my pace. After four months there, I became the manager. I was giving out my business cards. On the back of the cards, I would keep tabs of how many haircuts you had and after ten you got one free. I was the only stylist doing this job. I received a lot of clientele. I was doing a perm one day when my boss came in and asked me if I would talk to her in the break room. She discussed with me if I was using back bar products and giving them away. She said the inventory was off. She said it was me. I was fired. Meanwhile, my lady had the perm solution on her head and I left the break room quickly to remove this solution before her hair fell out. I told my manager that there was a lady I was working on and needed to get back with her and she just continued talking like she wanted me to screw her hair up. I knew just who the lady was that I worked with that would cause such havoc in my life. I hope she was feeling happy.

Some months went by and Brad won all the hearts of my friends and family. I was pondering what I needed to do. Brad was very supportive. He worked as an accountant. We continue to date.

Chapter Fourteen

I began to think I needed to open my own shop. I drove around the town looking for buildings for rent. Everything was about $1,100 to $1,500 just for 1,100 square feet. I searched for two weeks. One of my clients called me and asked if I had checked on a building on Highway 44 next to Eggberts restaurant. I told him I guess I missed that one. The next day I went to visit the people at the motel who owned the building. A lady came out and introduced herself as Carol. Immediately, we both laughed and realized we knew each other from college. I used to mentor her on the computer. I let her know I was interested in the building for rent. She handed me the keys and I went to look at the building. It used to be a salon prior to me (Helens Salon). They had all the equipment in there and all the supplies. Eight hundred square feet. I thought if an empty building was $1,100 a month and this one is full of all the equipment it's probably going to be just as much if not more. I left the building and went back over to the office. I explained to her that it was perfect but probably too expensive for me. She said, "$650 is too expensive?" I was floored. I said no ma'am I will take it. It was just two days later that I started my business and I called it Helen's Salon so people could find me from SmartStyle. It wasn't long before my business picked up and was going well and I was interested in hiring somebody for help. I played Christian music. I talked about the Lord in my business. God gave me the business so I thought I could give it back. Many things went on in my shop as far as moves of the Lord.

It was a sunny evening as I was closing my day at Helen's Salon. I was gathering trash to dump out back. A gentleman came who I did not know but had a bald head, so no haircut for him. I saw a white light behind him and I made my way to my counter. Introduced himself as Charlie and announced that I received the Reader's Choice award. I did apply but did not think I would be awarded this way. He handed me the award and shook my hand with congratulations. He asked if I had time for a chat. I cheerfully accepted. He then spoke that he heard of my salon and how it operated. He also told me he was a wrestler. He hangs around a bunch of dirty wrestlers that speak of things that should not be heard. We proceeded to talk about that topic, my salon, my son, and church eventually. He listened inattentively. I continued to inform him of the Lord Jesus Christ. Before our conversation came to a close, he gave his life over to Jesus. He looked as if everything was washed away and a fresh look was on his face. We concluded our conversation and he went about his way.

A couple of months later, he came and asked me to attend his wrestling event being held in our BOK building in Claremore, Oklahoma. I told Brad about it and he joined. Knowing what Charlie told me about the men and their demeanor I was a little uneasy about the event. But being that I was asked, I would make my way there with God's goodness and His protection on my side. The event was a little sickening. As their event finished up, Charlie introduced me to a few of his friends. I could see the hunger in their eyes for what Charlie had. I then pulled Charlie aside and said, "You know enough about the Lord Jesus Christ now that you can also introduce your friends to Him. If you feel uneducated, just pick up the Bible and read the book of John. That would be a good start." He answered that he would pray for them to be saved as well. As life went by, I saw Charlie time and time again. He still was doing really well for himself and still in the wrestling and newspaper business.

I can't help but wonder why the Lord puts us in mysterious places. Ones that you would feel you could not endure and the reason why is because there's someone who needs to be saved. I went on to receive two more awards. Three in a row.

Know the Lord enough to hear His direction. God wants you to succeed. Seek a Wrestling Match for Christ.

I found myself singing in the forest.

Brad surprised me with flowers at work. They were beautiful long stem roses, three of them and everybody couldn't help but smell them. The fragrance was breathtaking. At this time, we have been dating for a year and a half. The three roses I received on a Monday at work. On Tuesday I received six roses. On Wednesday I received a dozen, they were all in my office. Friday it was one red rose and a statue of an Angel and a card asking me out. Saturday night came and he was going to propose. He drove me to a place about thirty miles away and there was a waterfall so he said that we needed to see it. He pulled over on the side of the road because we had received lots of rain and the roads were flooded on the way there. He turned in his seat and offered the ring. I refused. This is not the way I wanted to have a proposal. I wanted it to be public. I even told him that. Days went by and he asked me to dinner. It was a quaint little restaurant out in the middle of the woods but very beautiful inside. While we were waiting for our dinner, he got up and got on one knee and asked me again if I would accept him as my husband. I accepted. The ring was absolutely gorgeous. It was a half a carat marquis and I loved it. It sparkled and I was so proud to wear it. Family, friends, church family and of course, Lee was very thrilled by this event. Fuzzy rejoiced.

My job was still thriving. I spent time making banners and making a new sign for the road. To get more clients, I would stand out in the median with a sign that said the haircuts price. People waved at me and honked as I was waving at them. News spread and before long, the newspaper came and did an article on me standing in the median. It was on the front page. Of course, this just boosts my business even more. I had people lined out my door.

I found myself singing in the forest.

Chapter Fifteen

At this time, I was still living in my parents' home. I could have rented a place but since they were gone most of the time, I felt no need. My neighbor across the street informed me that she was moving and was going to sell her home. I asked her how much and I guess it needed some work. A mobile home. I knew that Brad could afford that so I called him and let him know the situation. It wasn't long before I had a new neighbor. I thought it was perfect to have Brad living across the street.

A couple weeks later, he asked me to go look at a house that he was looking at for sale. He told me where it was at and after work, I drove down that street up and down and around and around looking for the house that he had in mind. I think I found it and I wasn't really pleased at the looks. So when I got back to visit him, I said that it looked nothing like a house that I would be interested in if that's what you have in mind. He said, "I think you looked at the wrong house." So we made an appointment to look on the inside. We drove to the house and he parked in the driveway and I started crying. There was a house that I was very interested in because my dream house was two-story and yellow with green trim. This house was only four years old at this time. We walked in and the carpet was hunter green and the walls were beautiful off white. The upstairs had a balcony that you can overlook into the living room and we had a fireplace. It was a four-bedroom house with three bedrooms upstairs. They used the bigger bedroom as a game room and television room. Twenty-seven hundred square feet. It wasn't long before I decided to move in with Brad.

My parents were home from vacation and were glad to get back home. Lee was in hog heaven. He loved the stairs, as all children do. It wasn't long before Lee said he wanted a dog. Just so happened at Thanksgiving a dog wandered into the yard to play with him and some friends. "Can we keep it?" I said, "It may belong to somebody and they were out of town for the holidays and going to be looking for him when they return." Two months went by and nobody claimed the dog. So he had a dog. His name was skipper and he was a white and red Jack Russell terrier. They got along very well and played quite often in the backyard.

I had a friend who was involved in Home Interiors and Gifts. She let me know how the business is done and wanted me to get involved. I invested $500 for my inventory. This would be one way to decorate my home. There were many meetings to go to and I learned all I could from each one. First, I did home interior shows and sales with my friends and family. You take your inventory which consists of votive cups, sconces, swags and pictures and arrange them in an attractive way and host a party. Try to sell your items even from a catalog. It seems in my life at this time everything I touched turned to gold. I blame it on the Lord spending so much time with me as I with Him. When I went to the meetings, I seemed to be the only one receiving free gifts and attention. One of the questions they would ask is how many parties we had booked. I always had the most. I enjoyed my job. I did this job on the side in the evenings and worked during the day at my salon. I also received a beautiful curio cabinet for all my dolls that I collected. I was so proud of myself. Having a business and knowing people was helpful, very helpful.

Chapter Sixteen

It was one month later, Lee was eight years old. Brad and I ran off and got married. April 28, 2000. Life went on and before long, we went shopping for the furniture that we wanted.

We found a kitchen table set in an advertisement dated three months earlier. We went looking for that kitchen table. A salesman came to help when we entered the store. We showed the advertisement. He said he had no more in stock. We went to another store and I did find the couch I wanted and it was on sale. I had an idea in my mind that the Lord had put there. Stop again at the first store. I told Brad there's something I need to do. I walked straight to the customer service counter. There was a lady there and I showed her the advertisement and asked her if she could help us? The salesman walked over saying there is no table. The lady looked frustrated at the gentleman.

She reached for an unadvertised merchandise catalog. She said, "Only one set left and it is $100 less than the advertisement." Thank you, Jesus, for guidance. It became ours.

Brad went to my aunt's estate sale. When I got home, Brad was very excited. He led me to the bedroom to see a very beautiful bedroom set in all pecan wood. A headboard, footboard, two end tables, tallboy dresser, armor and nine drawer dressers with mirror. Breathtaking indeed. He says, "I know you see there are no mattresses but I am trying to save the money to get them." He proceeded to say that "the mattresses were pretty brand new and because I knew that it was your family then I decided that's the ones I wanted. After buying this bedroom outfit, I had no money left over. I need $200 to buy the mattresses." We were both tight with money at this point.

The next day was Sunday (church day) and it was about 1:30 p.m. when we heard the doorbell ring. My dad didn't get out much especially by himself and there he stood staring at us with a smile. He wasn't known to be much of a Christian. He was raised catholic and kind of turned into a wild man in his young age. Drinking moments when I was growing up. He was harmless. He didn't have much to do with church. We asked him what he's doing at the door and what we can do for him? He said, "Well, I heard that you needed $200 for mattresses so here it is." He handed us the $200. As we visited a little longer, he didn't even come in, he left suddenly. Brad then said, "I believe God sent your father to give us that $200." We had a bed to sleep on that evening.

Jesus gives you everything your heart desires if you serve him first of all. It was a great night's sleep. Jesus always sets us up for improvement.

After two months of enjoying our new things, we wanted to purchase some land behind us. Two and a half acres.

It was a beautiful fall day. The leaves were a beautiful color. We lived in a fairly new housing addition. We were on a half-acre of land. There was an acre behind us and another acre and a half behind that which had no development. We were wanting to figure out how to buy that land.

As I was walking the dog one day in the neighborhood, a gentleman was at his mailbox. We struck up a conversation and they had bought the acreage behind their house. I asked him where and who to contact for the land. He gave me the information and I got to the house and told Brad about it. We called the number and set up an appointment with a gentleman. When he arrived, we all sat at the table, three of us. I sat across the table from the gentleman. As we were discussing the land outback, he informed us of the cost. The cost was $33,000 an acre. I can feel the Lord tugging me to ask for both pieces of land. I quickly asked about purchasing both pieces of land which was two and a half acres. He gave me a quote of $45,000 for both. With small thinking I said, "It is sold." We took care of the paperwork right there.

When the gentleman left, we began to laugh and rejoice. Later we found the land was worth $45,000 per acre.

He will move mountains. Walk in the ways of the Lord and you shall be blessed going in and blessed going out, all these things shall be added unto you.

I found myself singing in the forest.

I was working and my nephew came in to see me. He was twenty years old. He and Brad were working out in the garage trying to build their muscles for about a month and a half. He took me to the back because he had something to tell me. He proceeded to tell me that Brad was talking to him about sex. My nephew said he got up and left and came straight to me. Another bad sign for my marriage. When Brad and I arrived home, we both had a long talk. He said this was the only way he knew how to talk to him about this subject due to him not having a father. I disagreed. I was triggered with some mania after this event and this went on for about a month and a half. Mania grew. I was starting projects and not finishing them. I was losing things and frantically trying to find them. I would get stuck on a thought and not be able to get through it easily. I would fly off the handle. I saw a doctor, therapist. This is when I was diagnosed with bipolar 1. I was put on a medication called Effexor. I developed acne around my neck due to the side effects. Scars around my neck, a strangled look. The doctor and I had problems finding the right medication. Then, Latuda and Rexalti came along. I had to take both. This calmed things in my mind. Eliminates some of the mania. Made me almost numb. This gave Brad the upper hand as though I was the problem and manipulation made me think I was at times. My therapist was telling me that it would take time for me to adjust to the medication, I was depressed. On top of that, I had fibromyalgia. I discussed things with my family and they just looked at me with love in their eyes but never told me what I needed to do or to get away from Brad.

We had purchased a timeshare. It became of great value to us as we spent a lot of time on vacation. I had two ladies working for me now and they could hold the fort down just fine. We visited the Alamo in Texas, St. Louis, Missouri, and Branson's Amusement Park, Silver Dollar City. New

Orleans, Durango, Colorado, and experienced a hot air balloon ride. South Carolina, Washington, Cocoa Beach, Florida, California, the Pueblo Indian caves, Grand Canyon, Nashville. All of these vacations, I took a little piece of heaven with me home.

Chapter Seventeen

I went to work and wasn't feeling very well so I left and went home early. I laid in the bed and rested most of the day. I started moving around the house I had errands to run.

It was a long country road I was driving on when I felt a sharp pain in my side. I thought it was just hunger pains so I stopped for food. From that moment on each day, I felt the pain. I made a doctor's appointment. During the wait, I worried. As I visited with the doctor, he made an appointment to see a specialist in the digestive system. Many X-rays and tests were done. The news came that I had hepatitis C. This disease has to do with your liver function. When I got in my car, I began to pray. "Our heavenly Father, I know you are good to me and I am praying that you please give me the strength to endure what lies before me. Only you are the Lord who holds the keys to my future and I know that in your arms I will be safe through my journey." I drove to my parents' house. Another safe place. They always lifted me up in a time of need. As soon as I walked through the door, they knew there was something wrong. The one question was how did you get this? I had an eyeliner tattoo. That's the only relevant way I knew in my mind of how I received it. My mother and I prayed. I left to go home. My husband arrived soon. I told him there was a chance with some medication, ribavirin that was first coming out in October. The first medication was to be taken for three months. Lee took this a little hard. He was 15 years old. He took his teddy bear and put his head down as if he was crying. He hugged me and said, "Mom, everything will be okay." I believed him.

I had no side effects. After completion, I took some more tests and found the results to be the same. The doctor said there would be another medication coming out in January. I was forced to close the door to my shop due to my illness. It was a really sad day for me. All that I had worked for was gone. On top of feeling sick, I felt sick losing my business. I spent more time with my family, especially Lee.

Christmas came and it went through my mind that this might be the last Christmas that I'm able to spend with my family. At one of my lowest points,

I found myself singing in the forest.

January came, the news was that I had to take a medication called interferon for one year. It consists of needles in your stomach and it was a lot like chemo. I was frightened. I asked about the side effects and got the chilling answer of it's just like chemo. The medication left bruises in every pin-prick mark. I threw up. The weight loss and the hair loss. I went to sit in my car on the hill of the church that overlooked Claremore. The place I prayed while I was growing up.

After going through one year of torture, I knew that my family stood strong beside me. I did my best to stay strong. Lee was going through some bullying at school. I remembered how people would get cars in school and they were treated better depending on the kind of car they drove. Anyway that's what I saw in kids when I was growing up. My sister Fran had a convertible, in high school, and a good-looking boyfriend. So I bought my son a used corvette. Dark blue T-top. I believe it was in the '80s. Lee loved his games with Mario kart and games like that, I wouldn't let him play violent games. He loved to stay home and have his friends over. We had a pool table, four wheelers, travel trailer, mopeds and boat. All kinds of toys for children to play with. So believe it or not he didn't drive it very often only to work and school, the weekends he stayed at home. Something I wouldn't have done as a teenager with a corvette. He was a good son. He was very obedient.

The medication failed.

It was six months later before I was able to take another treatment.

Holidays came and went and each one made me feel like it could be my last. I had a brother-in-law who also had hepatitis C and he passed away from his liver failing. My liver wasn't doing so well either.

I spent a lot of time at the house because Lee and Brad were at work. I hired a housekeeper. I was that sick. Time came for the third treatment. What did I learn from this experience? The doctor was just the same. Seemed like the doctor just repeated herself but she did say the name of the new medication was Harvoni. This treatment lasted three months and it was by ingestion.

I had mild side effects and got to know my housekeeper very well. I spent time with my parents. It saddens me even worse to know that they were hurting due to my illness. This time my parents went with me to the doctor. Tests were done and I was waiting three days. They took me out to eat even though I wouldn't tell them that I was not very hungry due to the side effects. I ate everything on my plate.

Test was a failure again. Six months till new medication.

Just taking each day as though you were going through a field of flowers helped.

During all the time I was sick, I didn't miss a day at church. Everyone was so kind and prayed for me. It's good to know people care. As I was there, our friends were sitting with us. We didn't know them very well. We've just been acquaintances and had a few lunches together. At the altar call, they went to the front for prayer and they were down on their knees. As I prayed and worshiped, I saw a white light around them and heard a small voice in my head that went right along with my heart. The voice said, "Go down and pray with the couple on the altar and let them know their son will be home in three days." I thought this was a joke. I continued praising and worshiping as I heard the voice once again. I thought, Jesus, there are people's hearts that will be hurt and I will look like a fool. A few moments later, I heard the voice again. I left the pew and began to approach the couple. I got down on my knees and I prayed with them. I had no idea what to pray for so I just prayed the casual prayer. I have heard people say that the Lord can speak to each other and prophesy and then I've heard people say that it's not of God. I took the chance. I let them both know about the voice I heard and tied in with my heart and I was told to tell you that your son would be home in three days. They said that their son has been gone for six months and they have been praying for him to come home. Matter of fact that's what they were praying for at the time I arrived. They thanked me for the prayer and got up with hope.

Monday came again and it was another day. I'm thinking about my salon and how much I missed the people's visits. How the Lord touched people there. I lost my business and I told myself again. I couldn't understand why my Lord God let this happen. I was beginning to give up on hope.

Heartbroken, I had more time on my hands. I came home several times to have caught my husband having fornication with himself. He even asked me to join him once. No way. I found it to be very perverted. I found it to ruin my sense of woman-ship and I found myself to be unattractive. I found myself, well I was to the point where I couldn't even find myself anymore. I spoke to him about the event and asked him to go to counseling with me. We made an appointment.

The couple's son came home in three days. Praise the Lord and all that's within Him, praise His holy and lofty name.

We met with a gentleman who was our new counselor. When we got to the point of talking to him about pornography his answer was, "all men do it." Well, my husband looked at me and laughed and said, "There's nothing wrong with what I'm doing." My heart sank. I didn't know how I was going to handle this moment. I couldn't figure out how I was going to handle any moment past this. Our relationship became distant. Mainly because of me not understanding the whole concept. I felt that way. Brad began to belittle me often.

If someone treats you badly, just remember that there is something wrong with them, not you. Normal people don't go around destroying other human beings.

A divorce I wanted. Brad filed. I was now out of work and was pretty sure I was going to be out of a marriage. My parents were married for sixty-five years and I wondered how they did it. Next, I entered the garage to see a giant moonshine still. I proceeded to ask him some questions and Lee came in and said, "Mom, all he needs is a license. This is Oklahoma." Brainwashed. Manipulative. I turned around and made my way to the bedroom with some thinking to do.

It was two weeks later when I packed some of my things and moved away. Lee was 22 years old. I had no money, Brad had it all in his bank account. My parents were home but I didn't want to involve them. Lee and his Fuzzy were home from college for the summer. He had a full-time job and didn't quite understand what was going on between Brad and myself. I asked Lee if he wanted to join in leaving Brad and he refused. After my decision making of how I handled the leave, I'm glad he didn't go with me. The day I left, I had no idea where I was going to go and really didn't want to be around people so I slept in my car for two days at a QuikTrip store. It was pretty much the roughest thing I've ever been through in my life. I got desperate and took my rings that Brad bought me and went and pawned them. I still miss them today. When I got some money, I went and rented an apartment in Tulsa, Oklahoma. Not knowing what I was going to do in a few months when my rent became due again. As I came to Claremore a few weeks later, I started speaking with my friends. They were a little upset with me for not including them. I could not tell them everything due to the complications. Brad tried a lot of things to get me back. I was overwhelmed by everything. My health being one. I hit rock bottom. Depression set in.

My divorce was filed by Brad.

Chapter Eighteen

Are you from here? A gentleman asked while waiting in the waiting room at a DMV. Nice to meet you. When I returned back to the lobby, there he stood a brown receding hairline and about six foot three. Guessing his age, I would say he was in his fifties. I was now forty-five. He shook my hand to introduce himself again. He asked me to lunch. That is how it all began. Lots of laughs we had and it was nice to be able to have a good time again. He was kind, lovable, and very knowledgeable.

I asked him (Danny) for help. I let him know that I didn't know what I was going to do the next month. He wanted to help. I was waiting on a disability check for four years. Due to mental anguish which was bipolar disorder and fibromyalgia I never knew they were this severe till I went through a tragedy. I knew I had problems ever since I was a kid but never knew that there was a name for it. I did know one thing; I knew that many of my problems in my life were probably due to that. I couldn't pick the right boyfriends. I couldn't make the right decisions. And I surely couldn't make a relationship work. Danny was very helpful when it came to disability. He said, "How long have you been waiting for your settlement?"

I said, "four and a half years."

He said, "Have you sent in a doctor's report or have even made one?"

I said, "Make one?" I told him that I thought the attorney was taking care of that.

He said, "Attorneys will draw it out for five years until they make the maximum fee." He helped me get a doctor's report. He paid my rent for the next three months and he was very helpful at getting my paperwork together to receive my financial help. He was very smart. After sending a copy to Social Security, we sent a copy to my attorney. They were very upset at me for submitting my paperwork without their approval. I received my government check after my third month rent.

Danny and I often decide to get together for lunch. Our relationship grew from there on.

I still endured the pain and suffering of hepatitis C. The doctors are saying again, another medication is coming soon to help your symptoms.

We saw each other often. Soon our relationship grew strong.

We decided to move in with one another and he got me a moving truck. He only had a one-bedroom apartment and I don't know how we squeezed everything in there and still have room in it to live. What a difference from my previous life. All my 'toys' were gone. Anyway, I thought so.

My next appointment arrived for my new treatment. Danny was a good supporter when it came to this subject. We went into the office and she proceeded to talk to me about my situation, again. She introduced me to the new drug Savoli. I went home to consume my first treatment. It was a pill and was to last eight weeks. You took a pill three times a day. The first week was rough. I dealt with headaches and an upset stomach. Again, Danny was very helpful. That didn't stop us from doing fun things. We both like goodwill. We would go there and try to find some trinkets that were worth some money. Occasionally, we would get lucky. We went sightseeing. Oh, some of the scenes he showed me, and I returned the favor with some sites that I knew about.

Weeks passed fast. We went into the doctor's appointment, took some tests and left. It was five days later before we got the results. We anxiously waited. Soon we returned to the Doctors office for the results. I had high hopes. PRAISE THE LORD, I WAS HEALED! It took a long time for the right medication to come to the public but when it did, it was perfect. It felt good not to be sick anymore. It felt good not to have the pain in my side. The symptoms of Hepatitis C went away during my last week of treatment. I told my family, especially Lee. Yes, his teddy bear rejoiced! He has been a long-loved friend. One of the things that I desired in my life was to donate blood. Due to Hepatitis C, I will never be able to donate blood again. This saddened me.

When I met Danny, he was attending Life Church. I went with him. It was too loud. I didn't mean for it to, but it snuck in and stole my joy. Danny didn't like how they asked for money. Anyway, how they went about it that is. I missed my church in Claremore. I missed the nursing home ministry. I'm hoping to be able to get involved with the nursing home ministry again somewhere. Time will tell, I have faith. I was taught in the Assembly of God in Siloam

Springs, Arkansas to launch out into the deep, quit cleaning your nets.

My girlfriend Teresa, from Siloam springs Arkansas passed away in an automobile accident. She will be missed by plenty of people in her life.

Lee was still visiting and we were getting along just fine like nothing had happened. Thanksgiving and Christmas, we spent together. It was October 24 that he decided to tie the knot with a good-looking girl that he meant through a friend. Her name was Stephanie. They had a wonderful gathering at the wedding, at least on Lee's side. I guess Stephanie's family or friends were all involved in the wedding ceremony. There were only two people sitting on her side. Danny and I. There was no room on the groom's side to sit. The wedding was absolutely gorgeous, and it took place at Claremore Museum which has a beautiful landscape. The wedding was outside. It was a bit chilly, and I was uncomfortable with my ex-boyfriend, Lee's dad and Brad there at the wedding. I didn't know how to handle this situation and Danny wasn't much help. I went to Lee after the wedding and spoke to him about being uncomfortable and that I was going to leave. That was the stupidest moment I feel like I have done in my whole life. I should have not let them bother me. It was my only son, actually my only child. Bipolar-UGH! So many mixed emotions and I did not know how to maintain them. I take medication but it doesn't stop the thoughts completely. It just calms some moods down. Too many people. I wept in the car. Danny reassured me that I was doing a lot better with my episodes. We left. So sad for me. I was so sorry. Lee took it well as he knew I was struggling. He didn't hold it against me.

They went to Disney World on their honeymoon with the timeshare. When they came back, they came to visit so we could see the pictures and a visit about buying a house.

They were keeping Skipper in his old age. I was able to see him, and he was blind and wobbly. It was a couple of weeks later and he had passed away. He lived seventeen years. Good dog.

It was Tuesday evening when Lee and I were texting one another and somehow, we got into a conversation about Brad. The conversation was about him being the only father that Lee knew. My complaint was Brad's fornication. And he was going to still talk to him. I decided Lee was a grown man and can make his own decisions. It was soon after that we learned Stephanie was pregnant. Because they both worked full-time, I didn't get to see them much. We lived about thirty-five minutes away from each other.

Danny and I were still kindling our relationship just fine. He still had many things to talk about and I still had an ear to listen. Believe me, I had stories to tell too, and he had to listen to mine. It definitely was a two-way street. We still went on little trips.

Time went by fast and I got to go to the hospital to see my new grandbaby after she was born. Her name was Aimee. Beautiful little girl. She looked a lot like her mom but she had the cheeks of her grandmother. Oh, that would be me.

Danny needed surgery on his back. One-year wait due to Covid19. When I met him, he proceeded to tell me he's already had seven surgeries on his back and three on his neck. He used to be a boilermaker and fell inside and hit every ugly pipe on the way down. The doctors had to go through his stomach and threw his back for this surgery. I felt sorry for him as he walked around the house very carefully. Two months after the surgery he grew a shark fin like protrusion in his stomach. We went back to the doctor and asked him. They failed to reattach the stomach muscle securely. Of course the doctors didn't want to say that they messed up. Poor Danny, we had to have a second surgery. This is for the major hernia that they had created in his stomach from the previous surgery. The new surgeon said this was the worst hernia he's seen in 45 years of doing surgery. The hernia wrapped all around his body. They cut him in half, from one side to the other. We are now waiting for him to go in for a third surgery due to a few more rips that were not seen and taken care of at the time. He slept often and I got bored. Not sure how this writing would sound but getting it off my chest I found a healing process. So I grabbed a paper and a pen and I started writing a story of my life.

Chapter Nineteen

Lee, Stephanie, and Aimee met us at the Gathering Place in Tulsa, Oklahoma for my granddaughter's first birthday. The Gathering Place has all sorts of fun things to do for children and even adults. It was on 66 acres. Very popular and people drove from other states to come and see the Gathering Place. It was fun to watch my one-year-old Aimee go up and down the little hills which I knew to her seemed big. I couldn't get her to come to me though I guess because she didn't know me very well. Even Lee tried to hand her to me and she refused. The next day would have officially been her birthday. I called and asked if she was having a birthday party at her home. Lee informed me that they were having one but that's the reason he met me at the Gathering Place because he was inviting Brad. That upset Danny and I. Brad was around Lee for 16 years. I was around him all my life! No problems only with him treating me disrespectfully at times. I wasn't invited to the party. This led to an argument between me and my son. It lasted one year and two months. He began to send pictures on my phone of Aimee. Even some pictures of himself at certain pro football games. No texting or talking though, just photos. Slowly we are rekindling our relationship. I missed him so much. Four months before our relationship started, we found out that Stephanie was pregnant again and expecting a girl in one month. Her name would be Sarah. Five weeks went by and Sarah was born. My son sent a picture from the hospital. Again, this baby looked like her mom and my cheeks. We are still working on our relationship and it worked its way out all by itself. I let him know about things that's going on in my life. Things that are good things that are just and things that are true in the eyes of the Lord. I have an avenue to talk to him. I pray he will come around to visit with me once again. The divorce was hard on him and I think he blames me for it. By the way, he is an accountant just like his stepfather. I am very proud of him. He graduated from Oral Roberts University in 1991.

James chapter 1:6 perseverance makes us mature in our mindset and perseverance makes us complete in our character.

I wrote him a note and sent it in the mail. Never got a response.

"Please."

Let me share with you.

We used to play together. Diapers, bottles, teaching to walk, talk. Teaching to use the bathroom with Cheerios, taking you to daycare, to work with me, playing checkers, jacks. Taking you to all your games, but one. How to clean, do dishes, put up wallpaper, mow, social events, interact with family members. Sing, vacation, shop, bikes, church. Taught you how to love the Lord at a young age. Making Him your everything (including your father when you had none). Buying you a corvette so people would dote on you, gave you my Highlander, I drove my parents' old station wagon, such humility. Hiking and dental experiences, hernias, eye surgery, teaching you that boys don't wear earrings, and so much more before Brad. He didn't interact with you until your late teens. I say this to let you see how much a mother cares.

Danny has been the only male ever in my life who can keep me close in a relationship. He cares deeply.

Please understand and accept us. I love your family. I miss you all. Family is important for us all.

I am trying to appeal to the compassion that I know you have in your heart.

I am grateful for you. What can I do to make you understand how much I miss you? How can I help you to understand me?

I hope handling my illness is something you choose to do.

Well?

Love, Mom

Chapter Twenty

After receiving my check from Social Security, I had a pretty big settlement. Danny and I got married. Eloped in Branson, Missouri. We also were able to purchase a home, well a down payment. It was a double and a half size modular home. It was two thousand square feet. The space, that's what I needed to let go of my home through the divorce. It has a very spacious living room big enough for a sectional and still has plenty of room left. You walk up on a beautiful deck and go through the door, a red door, and you can see straight through the house from the living room to the kitchen into the far back room. The far back room we remodeled to be a salon. A styling chair, shampoo chair and a sink. All the equipment I needed to do the work that was before me. I have some clients that I still take care of and brought on some new clients through advertisement. Danny thought of my happiness. I have redecorated one room into kitty cats and a light post and beautiful curtains in purple. The other room is our office room and our bedroom are very spacious.

I lost the hot tub in the divorce. I lost a lot in the divorce but I'm finding myself again. Danny and I have found a church. I can't help but think of this song: Artist: We the

Kingdoms, 'Holy Water': "I don't want to abuse your grace, God, I need it every day. You're the only thing that ever really makes me want to change." Artist: Mercy Me: "We Win!" I desire church life. I enjoy nursing home ministry. I very much enjoy people.

Danny and I's conversations are never ending. He talks about how grasshoppers live and how ice boxes got started. A song reminds me of him. Artist: Brian Littrell 'Welcome Home You.' I learn a lot from Danny. He is a solution to a problem. We live life a bit slower now.

We have great neighbors here also. In Broken Arrow, Oklahoma.

It was a fair day. Valentine's Day. I was entering my neighborhood headed for home. I could see several of my neighbors smiling and waving as I drove by. I enter my driveway and Dax comes over to greet me as I exit the car with a look only a four-year-old could have. Excited to show me his new Spiderman costume. I was truly happy for him.

I walked to the community mailboxes. There were two neighbors having a chat. Bob introduced me to Mary and her husband Leon. They were new residents to the park. People were friendly by making eye contact and a hi. When I returned Danny was sitting on the front porch enjoying the afternoon. I went inside and the phone was ringing. It was my sister Julie. We talk every day for about an hour. We have communications about my other sisters at times. About Nellie passing away due to doctor complications and my parents passing six years after Christmas 2015. My father passed away two weeks after my mother. He said he couldn't live without her. And he didn't. Eternity is a very long time, especially toward the end.

Danny still suffers stomach pain and we are patiently jumping through hoops with the doctors. I went back to church, Assemblies of God here in Broken Arrow. Danny hasn't joined me yet due to his pain in his stomach. But I always come home and we talk about the lessons that I learned. We also listen to Charles Stanley together. One of our favorite pastors. My first visit was very accepting. I sat in the third row and was very excited about the songs they were singing. I raised my hands and gave praise to the Lord. After service that was taught on "Hope" I saw a lady approaching me. She knew I was new and asked me to a class she was attending after service. She asked me what my name was and I told her. She said it must have been a Divine appointment because her name was the same. I feel like the Lord put me right back on the elevator floor that I got off on. The next morning, I woke up to Pam walking her new dog. The day I was leaving to go to the grocery store, I opened the car door and on my seat was a rose. Oh, how I remember the day I received the rose on Valentine's Day years back. A special gift I received from the man upstairs. Now I have a man downstairs that treats me very well. Thank you, Danny, and many, many others and thank you Jesus for letting me know that you think of me and care.

I found myself singing in the forest.